THE COTTAGE

An American Gothic

ULTAN BANAN

THE COTTAGE

ONE

THE COTTAGE was nestled down a narrow lane strewn with the burned-ocher leaves of autumn. September was nearly gone and the trees that lined the secluded lane had almost fully shed, and dotted here and there among them were the pitch pines that would remain steadfast throughout winter. The day was still, the trees silent. The leaves on the ground did not stir. The car made its way slowly up the winding lane, the two occupants turning to admire each tiny home they passed. Sitting in the passenger seat with her hands clenched gleefully between her thighs, Katie turned to John, and smiled and bit her lower lip.

'It's dreamy,' she said.

John glanced over at her and grinned. He nodded, turning back to the road. He made a long slow right-hand turn and they saw it there in all its historic glory. They'd grown to know it and be familiar with it only from photos, and now, after two months, they were setting eyes on it for the first time. Katie's legs bounced excitedly and she suppressed a whimper of delight. She reached across the well of the car and put her hand on John's thigh and squeezed. He slid his hand onto hers.

The cottage was a shingled Cape Cod-style home with double dormers and a pilastered entrance. The place was surrounded by privet hedges and a white picket fence along the roadside, and rising above it from the back garden was a large oak that must have been three hundred years old. The place backed onto Pequot Woods, some 140 acres of protected woodland that was home to little more than marsh and hiking trails.

The car slowed and pulled into the drive, coming to a stop. John killed the engine and turned to look at Katie. 'Let's not get our hopes up until we've spoken to her.'

She leaned over and kissed him. 'Can we get just a little excited?'

He gestured with his head. 'Come on. Let's take a look around, shall we?'

He got out of the car and she followed. Approaching the window of the house, he cupped his hands against the glass and took a glance inside. She did the same.

'A bit sparse,' he said.

'But it's been vacant for so long.'

'Let's take a look around back.'

'Can we?'

'Of course. It's not like we're casing the place.'

They went down the side of the house to the white gate. John reached through and flicked it open and stepped inside.

'Are you sure?' she said.

He didn't answer and she followed him through. The garden ran for about twenty meters to the back hedge, the woodland beyond. In the middle of the garden was a large picnic table. To their left, by the gate, a small shed. Directly behind the house, a raised patio with the garden furniture still in its protective covering. Katie slipped an arm into his as they looked on, her other hand cupping her belly and stroking it gently.

'Can you imagine raising our child here?' she said.

He nodded, looking at the patio.

She looked off down the garden, gesturing with a movement of the head. 'A swing set down the back, and a paddling pool for summers,' she mused. 'Maybe we can open a gate at the back so we can go for walks together in the evenings, hmm?'

He nodded thoughtfully. She squeezed his arm. He wandered over to the back of the house to look through the glass doors of the kitchen. They heard a car pull up in front of the house.

'That'll be her,' John said. 'Come on.'

'I hope she doesn't mind us nosing around.'

They went back out through the gate where they saw the maroon sedan parked up behind them. The woman got out of the car and waved.

'Hey there. How are y'all?'

'Good.' Katie smiled, letting go of John's arm as he stepped forward and held out his hand.

'John. Pleased to meet you at long last.'

They shook. The woman threw her free hand in the air. 'Hell, I feel like we need no introductions anyhow. We've been talking for so long on the phone, it's like I know y'all.'

She shook Katie's hand. 'I see you've been having a look around?'

'I hope you don't mind,' Katie said. 'It's so pretty.'

'Not at all,' the woman said. 'Anyhow, if all goes as we hope, it's gonna be yours soon enough. Why don't we go and take a look inside?'

Inside, the hall was dusty and mail littered the floor. The house smelled musty and the woman immediately began opening windows.

'So sorry about this. It's been a while since I've been here. Marjorie and Elliot have been up in Providence for the last two years, and they've only been down twice in that time. Things get away from you, you know?'

'It's no problem at all,' Katie said. 'It's not even that bad. Nothing a sweeping brush wouldn't clear right up.'

John nodded. 'It's in great shape. It really is.'

'I don't wanna tell you how much money they pumped into this place,' the woman said. 'It's true, we got rid of some of the period features, but I'm all about comfort rather than style. I like my modern appliances, know what I mean?'

'Oh sure,' Katie said. 'I mean, just look at this living room...'

'As you probably saw already, the fireplace is on the gable end. But it's fully fitted with central heating. It can get cold down here in the winter, you know? You don't wanna be relying on wood. I'm not exactly the type to like things rustic, do you get me?'

'It's wonderful,' John said.

'Solid wood floors everywhere, except the kitchen, where they put down this gray oak laminate. But it wasn't cheap either.'

They walked across the room to the door and looked inside.

'Oh my God. It's so much more spacious than it seems in the pictures,' Katie said.

'Yep.'

Katie turned to John. 'Don't you just love it?'

'I love it,' he said.

'And just look at the view out the back...'

They all stopped by the double doors to gaze out. The woman opened the door wide and they stood in the cool air admiring the view over the garden to the woodland beyond.

'It's so idyllic,' Katie said.

'It is that,' the woman said. They were all quiet for a moment before she broke the silence. 'Anyone for coffee? I'm sure there's some in here, though it can't be all that fresh.'

No one answered, yet she went to the cupboard all the same and rustled inside until she found a Tupperware box. Taking it out, she opened the bag and sniffed it, and put it on the counter and took out a mug and began to wash it.

'You mind if we go look upstairs?' Katie said.

'You two go ahead. I'll be right up behind you.'

John followed Katie up the stairs. The upper floor was home to three bedrooms, two doubles and a single, one of the doubles en suite. A false ceiling hid the sloping roof, and being low, it retained the charm of days former despite its modernity. At the back, a small double, and at the front, the master bedroom. Katie slid a hand around John's waist as they stood in the door looking inside. He put an arm around her shoulder.

'What do you think?' he said.

'What do I think? I adore it.'

'As much as when we first saw the photos?'

'More.'

He kissed her on the head. Hand in hand, they walked over to the window and peered outside.

She looked up at him. 'This is the one, John. I felt it the first time I saw it. And I feel it even more now. This is it, our forever home. And now we've got the freedom...' She paused, turning to look outside. '...there's nothing stopping us. Right?'

She put her hand on his chest.

'Just this,' he said, placing a hand on her belly.

'I know. But it's only for a bit. Another five months and our child will be here. That's why I'm saying we buy now and go stay with my mom for six months until we have the baby. Mom can help for a little while, and then in spring we can move up.'

'I told you, Katie. I'm not staying at your mom's for six months. There's no way.'

'Aw, John...'

They fell quiet.

The woman appeared in the doorway behind them. 'Deceptive, ain't it? You wouldn't think this tiny place would hold three bedrooms. But I expect if you take it you'll be turning one of 'em into an office, huh? Nowadays everyone's working from home. There's gotta be at least one office.'

'John does, yes,' Katie said. 'I'm not working right now. I took a sabbatical when I found out I was pregnant. Doctor's recommendations, you know?'

The woman nodded. 'Sure, I hear ya. Gotta be careful. When's the young one due?'

'February,' Katie said.

The woman whistled. 'Middle of winter, huh? You planning to move right away?'

Katie looked at John. The woman held up a hand. 'That's okay, you don't need to answer that. I know these things are complicated.' She took a sip of coffee and joined them by the window. 'You wanna take a look out back?'

By the time she left, it had been shaken on. John promised the agent things would get moving before the weekend.

'I look forward to hearing from you,' the agent said. 'And call me if you have any questions at all.'

They said their goodbyes and got in the car and drove off, and in a half-hour they were on the highway.

'Can we do it?' Katie asked.

He squeezed her knee reassuringly. 'Course we can. We got this. Don't you trust me?'

'Of course I do. I just don't know why you can't agree to buy the place now and move in with my mother for a bit. It would be so much easier.'

'That's why we stopped off at the hospital before we dropped by the house, honey. To reassure you. Aren't you reassured? 'Cause you said you were.'

'I am. It's just, it'd be so nice to have Dr Erskine see out the pregnancy. She's been with me since I was a child.'

'And Dr Chaudri seems very qualified, don't you think? I got a very good feeling from her.'

Katie sighed. 'Yes, I know.'

They fell silent as they crossed Memorial Bridge. Katie turned to look out over the river. It reflected the silver-gray of the sky.

'I thought you two were getting along better,' she said.

'Your mom and I will never get along, Katie. We can be civil, but that's the height of it.'

'You could at least try.'

'Tell that to your mom. I do, I try plenty. But she's never gonna let up on me. Never. So please, let's just buy the house and move down as soon as we can get our hands on the keys. I can't face a week at your mom's, never mind six months.'

Katie said nothing, but rested her hands on her belly nervously.

'There's a Wendy's,' John said. 'Wanna stop before we hit the highway?'

'No.'

TWO

It was the 1st of November when the U-Haul pulled up outside the house. John opened the door to greet the guy, and after a few pleasantries, their worldly belongings were transferred into their new home.

'Quite a little pad you've got yourselves here,' one of the men said to John when the job was almost done.

'It's idyllic. My wife's been dreaming about it for a few years now.'

'Yeah, my wife dreams about a place like this too.'

'It's a bit of a gamble, but I think we can just about pull it off.' John raised an eyebrow.

'More power to ya I say.' The man nodded his head and turned to lift a box at his feet, pausing with it in his arms to look out at the husky hues of autumn beyond the window. 'Livin' the dream.'

When they'd gone, John caught Katie in the living room trying to lift a box.

'What are you doing? Put it down. You need anything lifted, you tell me.'

'Don't get in a twist,' she said. 'I'm not a whale just yet. I can still do stuff.'

'Yeah well, how about you concentrate on stuff that's not likely to do you an injury? Maybe something smaller? Leave the big stuff to me.'

'Fine.'

The sound of a car outside drew their eyes to the window.

'Oh look—Donnie's here.'

The couple went to the door and Katie rushed outside, throwing her arms around her brother. 'So great to see you,' she enthused, kissing him on the cheek.

John greeted him from the door. 'Hey Donnie.'

'John.' Donnie nodded, turning back to his sister.

'Hope you brought your toolkit with ya,' John said.

'S'what I'm here for.'

'Come on in we'll get you a coffee.'

With his arm around her brother, Katie led them into their new home.

'Well well. Isn't this idyllic.' Donnie whistled.

'Isn't it just a dream?' Katie said.

'It sure is.'

John lit the outside heater that evening and they sat on the patio and shared a bottle of wine. The night was cold but dry, and beyond their quiet conversation there was no noise to be heard but that of a distant generator. A few bats flew overhead but would soon disappear for winter. The forest, out beyond their garden, was still and implacable.

'Bit eerie out here in the evening,' Donnie said, zipping up his fleece.

'It's not so bad. I think it's just the isolation. No, not the isolation—the *space*. You know, coming from the city it's quite a change. From Queens to here it's a different world altogether. Sometimes I wonder if it's the same planet.'

'We just love the quiet,' Katie said. 'I mean, at first it's deafening, but it's growing on me, it really is. John just loves it.' She turned to her husband.

'Yeah, I sure do. Something calming about it.'

'You need to be careful it doesn't send you doolally,' Donnie said. 'It's kinda... vast.'

'It's only the great outdoors. This is the land this country was built on. A lotta history here.'

'Sure is,' Donnie said.

'We need to get some chickens, babe,' John said. 'I got my pregnant pilgrim wife here, all we need now is some corn and chickens.'

'Hey, I'm never gonna be that wife,' Katie said.

John smirked. 'No, I guess not.'

'Not our Katie.' Donnie shook his head. 'What're the folk like round here anyway? They're not ultra-conservative or anything, are they?'

'I guess many of 'em are like us,' John said. 'Got fed up with the city and decided to move down here for the quiet life. Right?' He turned to Katie.

She nodded. 'We met a few folk in town and they seem real nice. The locals, I mean. We haven't met any other exiles like us. Not yet. But I'm sure they're around.'

'What about that guy in the dollar store we went into for the cleaning supplies? He was a piece of work, huh?' John said.

'Oh God.' Katie raised a hand to her temple and twirled her finger.

'Some local hillbilly?' Donnie said.

'Yeah.' John shook his head. 'Tried to get us into his church within five minutes of meeting us, and got all pissy when we declined. One of these sanctimonious assholes, you know?'

'I'm sure they're not all like that,' Katie said.

'I hope not.'

'Sure if things get ugly you can always beat a retreat back to the city,' Donnie said. 'It's only a two-and-a-half-hour drive. No one'll think any the worse of you.'

'Oh God, not after the stress of this move. No, we're here to stay.' Katie sighed. John caught her glance longingly at his glass of wine and smirked.

'What do folk out here do for fun then?' Donnie said.

John chuckled. 'I'm not sure we're too concerned with fun. We've a kid on the way. Our hands are gonna be full. Next time we see fun it's gonna be, what, about twenty years in?'

Katie slapped him on the leg playfully. 'Don't be like that. Parenthood is fun too.'

'Says who?'

'Says generations of happy and contented parents.'

'Oh yeah. Those guys.'

'Someone sounds like they're getting cold feet,' Donnie said.

'No, he's not.' Katie rubbed John's leg. 'He's just got a touch of the nerves. Haven't you, dear?'

'It's all gonna work out,' John said. He squeezed her hand.

They fell quiet, turning to look as one into the darkness of the trees beyond the house, the flutter of the bats overhead a quiet reminder of the alienness of a country into which they were born but with which, deep down, they were little familiar.

'Hey, come look at this,' Donnie said from the kitchen. John and Katie wandered in from the living room where they were putting a coat of paint on the walls.

'There's a crawl space down here.'

Donnie was on his knees in the kitchen cupboard, where he'd uncovered a trapdoor.

'What the hell is it?' John said.

Donnie shrugged. 'Just a way down under the house. But it looks to be fixed up down there some. I can't be sure, I can't see anything—sis, pass me that torch will ya?'

Katie lifted the torch from the kitchen table and handed it to him. He flicked it on, leaning down into the hole.

'Well, I'll be damned.'

'What is it?' Katie said.

'I got no goddamned idea. It looks like someone began to fix it up for something, then gave up halfway. There's even lighting down there.'

'The estate agent didn't mention it,' John said.

'Likely she didn't even know about it,' Donnie said. 'Way down was pretty well covered up.'

'Wanna go down there and take a closer look?'

'Sure, I'm game. There's steps.'

'Are you sure you wanna go down there?' Katie said. 'There could be fumes or anything, you don't know...'

John shook his head. 'Don't be ridiculous. Fumes of what? If there was anything toxic we'd have smelled it by now.'

Donnie looked up. 'Shall we hop down, take a look?'

'Let's do it.'

The way down was by bolt-through steps drilled into the concrete blocks that formed the foundation of the house. The steps descended about eight feet into the crawl space below, which was a foot less than head height. The floor was filled and the walls bare concrete. Crouching, Donnie spun the flashlight around the basement.

'Weird.'

'Suppose it was used for storage or something?' John said.

'Hell if I know.'

His flashlight came to a stop in the corner. 'Would you look at that...'

'What is it?' said Katie from above, her voice heavy with curiosity. Neither of the men answered. They crept toward the corner where a hole about a meter square lay unfilled. Around it, the floor was blackened, as if at one point a fire had been lit there. Inside the hole, only the wet mud of the earth beneath. They both peered in.

'What's it for?' John shook his head.

'Now why in the hell would you leave a big damn hole in the middle of the floor like that? It makes no sense whatsoever.'

'Beats me.'

'It doesn't make any sense,' Donnie said again.

'Hey... shine your light down in the corner there.' John pointed and Donnie swung the light.

'What is that?'

John lay down on his belly and reached down into the mud, pulling out a little white bone-like thing. He rubbed it off while Donnie shone the light on it.

'A rabbit?'

It was a carving, in bone or maybe antler, about three inches in size.

'A jackrabbit, or a hare or something.' John said.

'Well if that isn't damned weird,' Donnie said.

'What are you guys doing down there?' Katie said from above, her voice tinged with worry. 'Did you find something?'

'I think we found bones,' Donnie shouted, then grinned at John.

'Don't...' John smirked. 'It's fine, babe. It's only a hole in the ground. It's nothing.'

'Are you sure? Don't play with me...'

'It's nothing at all.'

'Why do you suppose the ground's all black here?' Donnie said.

John shook his head. 'Your guess is as good as mine.' He turned to look around the space. 'Anything else down here?'

Donnie swung the flashlight. 'Doesn't look like it.'

'Well, come on we'll go up, before she freaks out.'

The two men shuffled back over to the steps and climbed up into the kitchen. Donnie shook his head. 'Well, now we know where the bodies are buried.'

'Shut up,' Katie said, 'and don't even go there.'

The two men grinned.

'I'm making a brew,' she said. 'Who's for coffee?'

Later that night they lay in bed in the dark, a dark never encountered in the city. Accustomed to years in the hubbub of a metropolis, the quiet that encompassed their new home was not yet conducive to sleep. Strangers yet in that alien environment, they lay inquisitively and introspectively, occasionally pulled from their private musings back into the comfort of each other's presence.

'What was that?' Katie whispered.

'That was an owl, babe.'

'A real owl?'

'As opposed to, what—a fake one?'

She slapped him lightly. 'Don't make fun of me.'

'Yes.' He smiled in the dark. 'A real owl.'

'I thought an owl went like, *twit-twoo*.'

'That's a cartoon owl. A real owl is more like *hoooo*.'

'Like we just heard?'

'Exactly.'

'Is it weird that I'm a grown woman who doesn't know what an owl sounds like?'

'No one who grew up in the city knows what an owl sounds like.'

'So how do you?'

John rolled over to face away from her. 'Because when we were little my parents used to take us out near Harrisburg where a relative of my dad's had a farm. We stayed there for three, four weeks at a time in summers.'

'And there were owls?'

'Yes, there were owls.'

Katie was quiet for a bit. 'How come I never knew that about you?'

'I hope there never comes a time when we know absolutely everything about each other.'

'No, I'm serious. Don't you think that's the kind of thing that might have come up in passing at some point already?'

John sighed. 'It was a long time ago. And nothing much happened when we were down there. I'd kinda forgotten all about it.'

'It's weird, that's all. That you didn't mention it before, I mean.'

'Now you know.'

'Yes, now I know.' She turned toward the window, noting the absence of light pollution beyond the curtains. Light and sound, and the absence thereof, was unsettling.

A low perturbing sound cut the silence.

'What's that?' she whispered.

'That's your brother, snoring.'

'Oh.'

THREE

Katie pointed at the little bone figurine that sat on the windowsill right in front of the kitchen sink, cleaned but still with traces of earth on it.

'What the hell's that?'

'I found it in the basement yesterday,' John said. 'Cute, huh?'

'Cute? It's creepy.'

'It's a jackrabbit. I thought it might be a nice memento of our new home. A mascot, know what I mean?'

'John, I don't like it. If you want a memento, can you put it somewhere I can't see it please?'

'Jeez Louise. Sure. I will.' He picked it up and slipped it into his pocket.

'Thank you.'

'No worries. Where's Donnie?'

'He went into town to pick up some stuff, wires or sockets or something.'

'Alright. Well, I'm gonna go chop some wood.'

'You're gonna do what?'

'I'm gonna chop wood.'

Katie smiled. 'What are you, *outdoors man* all of a sudden?'

John put his arms around her. 'I think it's about time we got that fire going, don't you? Think how sweet it's gonna be in winter when we got an open fire, and the two of us sitting in front of it, nothing but the crackle of the flames and the scent of wood smoke, and a bottle of wine...'

'Uh-huh. And me eight months pregnant. Very romantic...'

'There's still stuff we can do.' John grinned.

'Babe, how do you know the chimney's okay? I mean, there might be nests up there or anything. Shouldn't we get someone up there to check it or something?'

'Jesus Katie. What a way to kill the mood.' He sighed and slid his arms from her. 'It'll be fine. There's covers on the chimney. It's fine.'

'And where you gonna get the wood?'

'I'll go out back into the forest. Gather some.'

'It'll be wet, John. Even I know that.'

'No it won't.'

'And are you allowed to collect it, have you checked? Because there are regulations about these things.'

'Jesus, Katie. Just finish the dishes and let me do what I need to do.' He turned away. She stared at his back. 'I'll be back in a bit.'

He went out the back door, Katie watching him from the window.

Inside the shed he turned on the light, the door swinging on its hinges behind him. He looked around at his alien kingdom. It would take time, but eventually he would make it his. There was much that had been left by the previous owner, and much that could be thrown out. Hanging on the wall, rusted but up to the task, was an ax. John lifted it and rested it on his shoulder, going out the door.

The day was cold. He made his way down to the back of the garden where he explored the hedge for a way through to the woods beyond. He liked Katie's idea of putting a gate in to give them access to the woods. He'd do it as soon as he found time.

At the northwest corner of the garden he discerned a way through the hedge. Forcing the foliage apart, he squeezed through and into the dense trees just beyond their garden, coming out under the oak, the leaves of which were a deep golden orange. He picked his way through, the crackle and the rustle of the forest alive underfoot. He'd only gone a distance into the trees when he came across a fallen birch. He paused, looking down at it, then walked the length of it. The top of it was rotted with the remains of decaying mushrooms clinging to its trunk, but the lower end was solid. And it had been lying for some time, and likely the trunk was dried enough from the summer months. He'd need a woodshed, but he could easily put one up himself. He swung the ax, embedding it in the trunk, testing its solidity. He left it there, and looked out through the trees, his eyes unused to the kaleidoscope of greens and yellows, and reds and rustic browns. Hands on hips, he surveyed the land.

A flashing movement to his left caught his eye. He turned, but whatever it was no longer moved. Seconds later, he saw it again: a rabbit or a hare, he couldn't tell, quick and wild in the sharp light of morning. He tried to track its passage but it was soon out of sight. His hand slid into his pocket where it found the small idol. He pulled it out and looked at it, running his thumb over the peculiar carving. Having caressed it, he slipped it back into his pocket. He looked down at the ax and took a hold of the shaft.

'Jesus, you've been busy,' Donnie said later when he came out into the garden and saw the pile of wood on the grass.

'Wanna help me put up a woodshed?'

'If I've got time once I'm done with the wiring, sure. I gotta go Friday though, no question.'

John nodded. 'Sure. We'll see.'

Katie appeared at the back door. 'Hey, you guys wanna come in for something to eat? Lunch is ready.'

'You betcha.' Donnie took off his jacket and stepped inside. John sunk the ax into the block that lay at his feet and followed Donnie in.

'Go wash your hands please.'

'Yes momma.' Donnie chuckled. 'Looks like you might have one of them pilgrim wives after all, Johnny Boy.'

'I'll do what I'm told for the quiet life.'

Katie scowled. 'Like you ever do what you're told.'

When they'd washed and sat down, Katie put the pot of soup in the middle of the table and joined them.

'Should we say grace or something?' John said.

They both looked at him. Katie raised her eyebrows. 'I thought you were joking there for a minute...'

'What? It just feels like it's the right thing. You know, out here in the home of our pilgrim ancestors.'

'You've never said grace so long as I've known you.'

'First time for everything.'

Donnie held up his hands. 'I'll do the honors,' he said. He closed his eyes. 'Good bread, good meat, good God, let's eat.' He opened his eyes and smiled.

'That'll do just fine,' Katie said. 'Let's eat.'

After dinner Donnie opened a bottle of whiskey he'd picked up in town. The two men hit it energetically. And as they grew tipsy, John noticed Katie's increasing exclusion.

'I wish you'd think of me,' she said when he asked her if she was alright.

'Oh come on. We're just having a couple of whiskies.'

'And of course I can't.'

John gave a long slow nod. 'This is the sacrifice you have to make. I don't know what to tell you.'

'And what about your sacrifice, huh? What are you compromising for this baby?'

For once John had an ally. Donnie waded in. 'Come on, sis. I'm sure if John had a baby growing in his belly he'd be just as considerate as you are.'

'Would he?'

Donnie grinned. 'Yeah.' He turned to John. 'Right?'

'Of course. No way I'd put my baby's health at risk.'

'No? Well I have to lie beside you in bed all night, with your dirty whiskey breath. How's that for considerate?'

'Aw baby. That's not gonna do the child any harm.'

'And what about me? It doesn't do me any favors.'

'Lighten up, babe. It's been a hard day. I just wanna relax.'

She rolled her eyes. 'Of course. All that wood you chopped, mountain man.' She caressed her bump.

'You telling me you don't love that fire?'

She turned to gaze at the fire. She couldn't deny it and she said nothing.

'Uh-huh,' John said.

'You know what? I'm feeling pretty sleepy. I think I'll go up to bed.'

'Don't go, sis.'

'Naw, I'm really tired. Really. I'm gonna go lie down.' She struggled up out of the seat and walked between them to the door. 'Just promise me you won't be up drinking all night.'

'Promise,' John said, lifting a finger to brush her hand as she passed.

'See you in a bit.'

'Night, sis.'

She left, closing the door behind her.

'Hard to keep em happy, eh?' Donnie said when he was sure she was out of earshot.

John shook his head but didn't reply.

'Tough time for a woman though. Carrying all that weight around. And the mood swings. And the hormones and everything. Tough time.'

'Sure is.'

'You'll be alright. We had it bad, Jenna and I. I mean her. Me too, I guess. I was the one living on the other end of it. But yeah, you just gotta be patient. And do what you can to keep her happy.'

'I know.'

John sipped his whiskey and looked at the fire. A fine thing, something built with one's own hands. Even something as transient as a fire. He looked at his glass, turning it in his hand.

'Hey, you ever made your own booze?'

Donnie chuckled. 'What, you gonna go full pioneer on us?'

John shook his head. 'Just wondering. Why the hell not?

Can't be that hard, can it?'

'Knocking up a batch of firewater should be easy enough. Not sure how you'd fare trying to replicate that single malt.'

'Might give it a shot while I'm up here, know what I mean?'

'You just let me know when it's ready. I'll be up here like a shot with my tin cup.' Donnie laughed long and loud. He looked up at the ceiling. 'Hey is she right above?'

'Nah, we're the other side of the house.'

'Good.'

The two men looked into the fire, and it was a while before either spoke again.

When Donnie had gone off to bed, John went out in the garden for the night air. All was quiet. A solitary bat flew overhead and disappeared. A cigarette would have been just the thing, but he didn't smoke anymore. Nor would Katie have put up with it. She'd have smelled it a mile off. Instead he took a lungful of the night air and stepped out onto the grass. He stopped by his wood pile to admire it. It was a fine pile of wood. He looked up at the sky, figuring it wouldn't rain and that there was no need to find a tarp to cover the pile. Sure, it might be wet with dew in the morning but that would be no trouble. Yes, it was a fine pile of wood, and soon it would reach to the roof of the shed.

He walked down the garden to the hole in the hedge and squeezed through, stopping just beyond the hedge to admire the wall of forest that rose up before him. His hands went into his pocket. The jackrabbit was there still and he took it out, rubbed it and peered at it in the darkness, the little idol white and smooth in his hand. Out of nowhere, and through no volition of his own, a word came to his throat.

'Mowtukas,' he whispered.

Frightened, he peered into the darkness around him. The alien utterance that had spilled from his lips alarmed him. And the tone of his voice, the resonance of it, the very molding of the word, alarmed him still more. The voice was not his nor one known to him. It seemed to ring with the cimmerian pitch of the forest itself.

'Mowtukas,' he whispered again.

A chill ran through him and he flung the rabbit into the woods. Shaken, he climbed back through the hedge and went inside. Ten minutes later, he slipped in next to his sleeping wife. Outside the window, the cant of an owl spoke of the depths of night.

FOUR

'Lᴇᴛ's ᴛᴀᴋᴇ Donnie out for breakfast before he goes, what do you say? We haven't been out in town yet, not really. Might be a good opportunity to explore,' she said.

'Sure.'

'Great.' She smiled and kissed him. 'We've done the right thing, haven't we? Moving down here I mean. We're right where we're supposed to be, aren't we?'

John looked at her quizzically. 'Of course. What's the matter? Are you having doubts?'

She shook her head. 'No, not at all. I just woke up with this weird feeling, you know? Like, I dunno what it was. Maybe just a weird dream. It's nothing. Really.'

'You sure?'

'I'm sure. Come on. Let's go have a nice breakfast and say goodbye to my brother.'

They drove over to Shaffer's Marina. At a bar-kitchen overlooking the harbor, they sat at an outside table despite the chill. It was sunny. Donnie sat with his shades on, admiring the view over the harbor and out beyond over the water.

'This is a life I could get used to,' he said, arms folded.

'Not bad, eh?' John said.

'Hell yeah. This is some spot. Place is a bit of a ghost town though, huh?'

'I guess at this time of year after the tourists have disappeared things get quiet.'

'Shit yeah, they do.'

'That's why we're here though, isn't it?' Katie said. 'Isn't this what we've been dreaming of for the last three years?'

'Sure is,' John said. 'This is definitely our dream.'

A waitress came and took their order.

'Lobster roll? At ten in the morning?' Katie grimaced.

Donnie smiled. 'Hell yes. You don't get these in New York. At least not like they make 'em here.'

Katie shook her head. 'I think lobster would make me hurl right now.'

'Thank God I'm not pregnant then.'

When the waitress returned with their coffee, Katie asked for a shawl.

'Just to take off the chill, you know?'

'Oh sure. I'll be right back with one.' The waitress went inside.

'So, think you'll take to this quiet life?' Donnie said. 'Sure is dead around here.'

'Oh sure.' John sipped his coffee. 'It's only a few months to spring anyway. And by February we'll have another little soul to keep us company, right?'

Katie massaged her bump. 'We'll be a family. A real family.'

Donnie grinned. 'Bet the first thing she wants when she comes out is a lobster roll.'

'Oh God...' Katie rolled her eyes. 'The first thing I'm gonna want when this is all over is a lobster roll.'

'And a vodka,' John added.

Katie sighed. 'And a vodka.'

The waitress returned with a shawl. Katie took it and wrapped it around her shoulders, and picked up her tea and cradled it in her hands.

'Hey maybe next time I come down here you'll have your own little boat out there in the harbor, what do you think?' Donnie lowered his glasses and peered at the boats dotted in the water.

'That's one thing the bank manager isn't gonna sign off on this year,' John said. He looked at Katie. 'Maybe in another few years?'

She said nothing, only raised her eyebrows enigmatically.

'Hell, maybe I'll buy one and dock it down here.'

'I doubt Jenna's gonna go for that,' Katie said.

'Well, let's not tell her.' Donnie grinned.

'We'll see how long that lasts.'

'Women don't need to know everything. Am I right?' He turned to John.

'A boat's a pretty big secret, Donnie. Maybe start with something smaller.'

'Hey are you opened all winter?' John asked the waitress as she cleared the table.

'We are. But we don't open until four in low season.'

'When's low season start?'

'End of the month.'

'I see. Hey can we get the bill?'

'Sure. I'll bring it right over.'

Donnie sighed and patted his belly. 'That was swell, guys. Thank you. And not to skip on the bill, but I need to be getting on. I gotta be back for four.'

'I told you, I got this. We're both extremely grateful for the help you've given us this weekend.'

'Nothing at all, guys. Anything for my lil' sis.'

He stood, came around the table and put his arms around her. Kissed her on the cheek. She patted his arm then rose to hug him.

'You better be back down soon.'

'You bet I will. There's a table right here with my name on it.'

'We want you to come see *us*, and not just to pick up a sandwich.'

'Two birds, one stone.' He grinned. He turned to John. 'Hey you take care of my sis, you hear? And my little nephew.'

'I will.'

The two men shook hands.

'Message me when you get back,' Katie said.

'I will.' He kissed her a final time on the cheek. 'Love you.'

'Love you too.'

He waved and descended the outside patio, heading for the car park. John and Katie sat down.

'He's a good guy, your brother.'

'He is.' She wiped a tear from her eye.

'You okay?'

She shrugged. 'Yeah. It's just the hormones.'

The waitress returned with the bill and laid it on the table. John picked up one of the three little white chocolates that sat on the tray. Rabbit-shaped.

'Hey what's this?' he said.

The waitress looked at his hand. 'Oh that's just a little chocolate from us. On the house.'

'No, I mean the rabbit—does it mean something?'

She shrugged. 'It's just a tradition we have around here. Doesn't mean anything. It's a chocolate.'

She walked away. Katie looked at John. 'What's wrong?'

'This thing—it's the same shape as the carving I found in the basement. I mean, *exactly*.'

'What, the weird little rabbit thingy?'

'Yeah.'

'I thought you were going to get rid of it.'

'I did. I threw it away.'

She shrugged. 'Must just be a local thing, like she said.'

He put the chocolate back on the tray.

'You don't want it?'

'Not hungry,' he said.

'Come on then, shall we get back?'

'Sure. Let's go.'

Arm in arm, they went back to the car. Stopping at the driver-side door, he dipped his hand into his pocket for the keys. He froze, pulling the carved idol from his pocket, and stared in disbelief at the thing in his hand.

Katie looked at him across the roof of the car. 'What? What is it?'

'Hmm?' He looked up. 'Uh, nothing. Nothing.'

He shoved it back in his pocket and pulled out the keys.

Back at the house, he set the car keys on the table in the hall. Katie took off her coat and hung it, and changed into slippers.

'Coming to sit down for a bit? I'm exhausted.'

'I'm gonna go get some wood for the fire.'

'Right now? There's a full bucket next to the fireplace.'

'We'll need more when that runs out. I'll go get some now. Want me to make you a tea before I go?'

'I'll be fine.'

She went into the living room and dropped into the couch. He changed into a fleece and went out into the garden and into the shed. Once inside, he took the jackrabbit carving from his pocket and turned it over in his hand. His tongue flicked over his teeth. He chewed his lower lip. He set it on the bench and looked at it, then glanced out the window, and went outside and looked down the back of the garden. Stood with his hands on his hips. Scratched the side of his face. Went back inside.

'You cheeky little fucker,' he whispered.

He picked it up and pocketed it, lifted a shovel and went out. He went out through the hedge and into the forest, a ways into the trees to the foot of a beech where he began to dig. When he'd dug about a foot down, he took the idol from his pocket and dropped it in the hole and stood looking at it for a moment or two. He shook his head. Then he filled in the hole.

When he came back up the garden, Katie was at the kitchen sink. She opened the window.

'Where were you? I thought you were getting wood?'

'I'm gonna do that now,' he said.

'What's with the spade?'

'I had an idea I might dig for mushrooms.'

'In November? You find any?'

'Nah.'

'Uh-huh.' She closed the window. He went and retrieved the ax.

'Come closer,' she said.

He slid closer. Put his arm around her. Around her belly. She took his hand and placed it on her breast. She nestled close to him.

'Hold me.'

He held her. He felt the warmth of her body and discerned her soft wordless advances. When he didn't respond, she took his hand and placed it between her thighs.

'Really?' he said. 'Isn't it getting a bit, you know, close? I mean with the baby and all.'

'No. No, it's not too close.' She turned to him. 'Kiss me.'

He kissed her in a way he had not since they'd left New York; indeed, in a way he hadn't since back when the baby was conceived. He kissed her and caressed her and nibbled her ear, and when she was wet he pulled up her nightie.

They lay belly-to-back post-coitus, a gentle sweat on arms that protruded from the duvet. Two bodies, warmth enough for each other on a cold night. Two bodies, three souls, for soon there'd be another. They lay in warmth and in the knowledge that within one of them a life spawned, knowledge that was in the heat of the bed and in the beating of a tiny stray heart, and in the hopes and fears for the circuitous journey of parenthood. All love, dread and the unknown contained in a single grasping embrace. He kissed the back of her damp neck.

'Do we have any pickles?' she said.

'You want pickles?'

'I want pickles.'

'It's the middle of the night and we've just made love. Don't be disgusting.'

'John, I want pickles.'

'Okay. I'll get you some pickles.'

'And bring my belly butter up when you're coming.'

'Belly butter. Right.'

He got up and put on his gown and went downstairs.

'Belly butter. Of course she needs belly butter.' He went to her pharmacy bag which sat on the kitchen counter in the dark and opened it and took out the tub of cream. 'Belly butter.'

Then he went to the fridge. His hand on the door handle, before he'd even opened it he discerned by some ancient sense the thing he had hitherto tried to cast away and which now sat inside, and that it was a thing of terrible beauty which betokened more than he could fathom but he felt in his gut nonetheless, a terrible thing, a relentless and corrupt thing, a thing he had taken into their lives or perhaps had stolen in. A thing which would not now leave them be until it had fulfilled some malign purpose.

He opened the door of the fridge. His skin was clammy and he trembled. It looked at him from next to the milk. His eyes glassed over as he reached out to take it.

'Mowtukas,' he whispered.

FIVE

THEN APPEARED another. Out in the woods with his ax a few days later, he found it nestled in a cavity in an oak, a small carved idol of a fawn, just like the other in bone or antler. He stared at it for a few seconds. Perhaps his eyes deceived him. But they did not. How could he not but think it was for him? That it was he it awaited, nestled there in the silent oak? He took it from the tree and put it in his pocket. He went back to chopping wood, unafraid but with a sense of inevitability growing in him that fate had taken him there, to that lonely corner of an ancient world, that cottage, those woods. That tree. Deep down he knew and could only relent to the hand of whatever power had guided him there.

He put it in the shed with the second, on an upper shelf where Katie might not stumble upon it. He obscured them with an old tin of paint and closed up the shed, and having gone back inside, at once forgot about them.

'You almost ready?' Katie said when he went in.

'Sure. Just give me a minute to get changed and we'll go.'

'Okay.'

He ran upstairs and changed quickly, and when he got back down she was waiting with her bag at the door.

'I'll just put my shoes on.'

'Sure.'

They drove fifteen minutes to Lawrence Memorial in New London and made their way to the Family Wing where they found Dr. Chaudri at reception. She greeted them warmly.

'Great to see you again. Back today for a scan?'

Katie nodded. 'Yeah. I can't have enough of these check-ups. I'm just a born worrier.'

'You got absolutely nothing to worry about. Dr. Erskine sent over your files and I've been over them this morning, and honestly, everything looks good. We'll give you a scan today just to make sure, but I don't foresee we'll encounter anything new. Best to be safe though.'

'That's her mantra,' John said.

'It's a good mantra.' The doctor smiled. 'Why don't you follow me.'

She led them down a corridor to an examination room and the doctor put Katie on the bed. John sat next to her. A masked technician nodded a greeting.

'I'll leave you with Clara here and when you're finished someone will bring you to my office. They'll send the scans right up.'

'Okay. Thank you Doctor.'

She left, and the technician picked up the gel. 'Are you okay to get started?'

When they were done an orderly brought them to Dr. Chaudri's office. They sat across the desk from the doctor as she turned to the computer.

'Right then, let's see what we have...'

John slid his hand into Katie's.

'So how long have you been down here now?' the doctor asked.

'Just a few weeks,' John replied. 'Still settling in.'

'You're brave, moving down here right before you give birth. And to your first. It is your first, isn't it?'

'It is,' Katie said. 'It's all a bit scary.'

'I'm sure. How's your new place?'

'Oh, it's just wonderful. It's a dream come true.'

'We get a lot of people coming up from New York. Don't

get me wrong, I love the city, but I couldn't live there. My sister lives there and wouldn't move for the world, but I could never.'

'We were there for almost four years. It was enough. We were really ready to move, weren't we, dear?'

John leaned back in his seat. 'Yeah, it was time.'

'Are you finding your way about okay?' Dr. Chaudri asked.

'Yeah, we're getting there, getting into the swing of things.'

'John's turned into a woodsman. He's never out of the forest. Loves chopping wood.'

'Oh yeah? Sounds great. I wish my husband was more like that. More practical. He just sits in front of the fire and reads. We get our wood delivered.'

'Like a normal person,' Katie said.

'Hey...'

She squeezed his leg.

'So, I'm looking at the scans and everything looks normal from here.' She turned the monitor so they could see. 'See there? The head, here the little hands...'

Katie turned to John. She gave a little tilt of the head.

'...here the feet. Looks great.'

'Are we...?'

'You ready to know the gender of the child?'

Katie looked at John. 'I think we are. Aren't we?'

He nodded. 'Yes. Tell us and put us out of our misery.'

'You're gonna have a little boy.'

'Oh John...' A tear ran down her cheek and she wiped it away. He put an arm around her.

'Congratulations,' Dr. Chaudri said. 'It so special, the first.'

'A son,' John said.

The doctor nodded. 'Right now you're carrying a beautiful healthy baby boy. And things should stay just as they are. I'm a little concerned though that you look pale, Katie. Let's get you some blood tests before you go—just to make sure, okay?'

'If you think I need it, Doctor.'

'Let's do it. To be on the safe side.'

They took a blood sample and the doctor told her she'd be in touch in a day or two.

'I can't thank you enough for all your help. We were worried coming down here about switching doctors and the care facilities and all, but we really needn't have. You've been amazing today.' Katie shook Dr. Chaudri's hand.

'Nothing at all. Here, take my card. If you need anything, just get in touch.'

'Thank you so much.'

'Thank you, Doctor.' John shook her hand and the doctor saw them to the front doors.

'See you in four weeks.'

'Thank you again.'

John put an arm around Katie and squeezed her shoulder. They shared a look as she cupped her belly.

'We better get back to talking names,' he said.

'Edward. He's gonna be called Edward.'

'After your dad.'

'After my dad.'

'I'm gonna light a fire, honey.' John took his jacket off and hung it.

'That's a great idea. You mind if I go up and take a bath?'

'Of course not. You go right ahead.'

'Thanks.' She kissed him on the cheek. 'I'll not be long.'

'You take your time.'

She took off her shoes and went upstairs, and John went out the back and took in some wood. He sat down in front of the fire, stacked the kindling and set it to light, and when it was going he stacked up the smaller blocks of wood around the flame. It took hold in the center and spread, the flame a trickle at first then a hot thrum that engulfed the fireplace.

John watched, saw the wood blacken and crisp, saw the red riot of the flame and the blue smolder that rolled across the surface of the blocks, and heard the cracks of the wood that sounded like shots in the forest, tiny explosions that spoke of silence around fires on foreign shores where hostile beings lurked. Long nights staring into fires wondering if the light of day would rise on one's poor and insufficient abode or if that night would be the last and no more would the earth's light warm one's back in morning, the fire the last light and warmth to be enjoyed in a land where time is marked in months, not years, the fire the measure of man's allotted time on earth. Should the fire go out, so too the life of man cut short. Fire was the first, the first of man's energies, for it came before food and it came before water, the whole earth forged in fire long before man set foot on the blackened rock. Did not man worship fire as a god? He did, and the roots of that worship remain. Proof of this is in the contemplation of the holy flame. Man saw the holy flame and knew he was in the presence of some other power that manifested itself beyond him, from realms he could not and would never understand. Raise the idols. Paint their glory on the walls so they may be remembered for eternity. Behold, the untold power of the gods of the burnt earth. The gods gave and the gods were generous, but man could not understand when they gave with one hand and took with the other, for with abundance came famine, and with rain drought, and with health disease. All things were given and taken away, but if man had fire, and man had water, he might live yet. Not only warmth but hope lived in the fire, the fire that lit the dark circle around which the embittered and embattled party crouched, twas the fire that drove away the desperation and the deprivation, and even the desire for death—

John?

—the desire that lives in us all, the counterpart to the will to live, which is the will to death, for dying is always easier than living. Passaconaway knew it as he crouched around his fire in the woods, the fire in a pit that they might not come to know of his whereabouts, that in sleep he might become Hobomok and deliver the land of the invaders, and if was decreed, do so by fire—

John?

—fire that the gods had given for such a purpose—

John felt the hand on his shoulder.

'John?'

He looked up to see Katie stare at him.

'Where the hell did you go? It's like you were a million miles away...'

'Uh, sorry... I dunno. I was just staring into the fire. I guess I drifted off...' He looked at the fire and back at her. This time he saw worry in her eyes. 'It's nothing. I swear, I'm fine.'

'You sure? Because if not, you'd tell me, right?'

'Of course.' He patted the hand on his shoulder. 'Don't worry.'

'Okay. You want a hot chocolate?'

'Sure.'

Came the first visitation.

The night was silent and cold. They slept deep and sound in the warmth of their proximity, but beyond, beyond the bed and the house and woods, something lurked. Something drawn to that place, to that locus of bygone woes. It slithered through the woods. It crept into the house, it crept up the stairs. Into the bedroom. It stood at the foot of the bed and watched. It climbed onto the bed. Stole over the covers. Onto her. It smelled her hair, it touched her face. It pulled back the covers to look at the rise and fall of her breasts. It could smell the baby inside her, the young life that budded in her womb. It put its hands and ear to her belly to better discern the beating heart within. Placenta. Aqua vitae. The ethereal beating of young veins. The first sighs of an earthly life heard through the river of her waters. One soul contained within another, and what is more nourishing than an infant soul? The being slid up until it was over the woman's face. It raised its hand and pushed two black fingers into her mouth. She opened her eyes and saw its face. Its face was like melting black-and-white plastic and it smelled of burning. Her eyes opened in surprise, then alarm, then terror—

She tried to scream. She fought in vain to swing her arms.

The scream still caught in her throat. It placed the other hand over her eyes

Katie... Katie...

He shouted. 'Katie!'

She awoke screaming.

'Jesus, it's me—it's me John... what is it?'

Lost, cowering against the headboard, she looked around the room, then at him. Her eyes were wide with terror. She was still fighting him off with her hands. He restrained her.

'It's me, Katie, it's *me...*'

Her hand came to rest on his arm. The touch released her terror and now a flood of tears came to her eyes.

'Jesus, John...'

'What? What happened?'

She spoke through sobs. 'It was on the bed, it was on me...'

'What was?'

'This thing, this black thing...'

'It was a dream, sweetheart, just a dream. I'm here, it's okay.'

'Fuck, it felt so real. It was on top of me...'

She broke down and said no more, one hand on her belly, the other wiping her eyes.

'You want a tea? Want me to get you a tea?'

'Don't leave me. Please don't leave me.'

'Okay. Okay. I'm not going anywhere.'

He put his arm around her, feeling the violent trembles of her body.

SIX

THE MORNING was quiet and there was little conversation between them. The night had left the house cold, despite the roaring fire that now burned in the living room. Katie sat wrapped in a shawl on the sofa, John next to her. Her stony mood was heavier than he could bear.

'I'm gonna go do a few hours' work. Can I get you anything before I get started?'

'Stop talking to me like an invalid.'

'I'm just trying to be considerate.'

'I know you are. But it's the way you say it. It's like you think I'm terminally ill.'

His hand slid toward her leg but he thought better of it. 'You know I don't mean to be condescending.'

'Clearly you don't mean it, John. But it's in every word you utter.'

'I'm sorry.'

Silence. He stood up, pausing for a second before going to the kitchen. He made a pot of tea and cut some fruitcake, put it out on a tray and brought it to her. He set it on the coffee table.

'Just in case you want something.'

She didn't reply. He left, went to the office, turned on the computer and sat down.

Work didn't come. The mood wasn't on him. Instead, he

opened the search bar of his browser. He glanced over his shoulder at the open door, before turning back to the computer. He typed in 'Mystic CT history'. It wasn't long before he was down the rabbit hole. Time slipped away, and he'd no idea how long he'd been reading when he heard her over his shoulder.

'Busy?'

'Hmm?' He changed tabs on the browser before turning around to look at her.

'Are you in the middle of something?'

'Nothing that can't wait.'

'Wanna go do something?'

'Like what?'

'I dunno. I just feel like I need to get outta here.'

'A walk?'

She shrugged, arms clasped about her chest. 'Sure.'

'Alright. I'll get my coat.'

He got up and put on his coat and she got dressed, and when they were ready he gestured toward the back door.

'What? Where are you taking me? When I said I wanna get out, I didn't mean the garden.'

'Let's go into the woods. It's beautiful out there right now.'

'John, I'm over six months pregnant. You wanna take me into the forest?'

'The woods. It's not the jungle, Katie. Just trees. The forest floor is nice and soft with dead leaves. There are even paths.'

'I don't wanna have to be clambering over any dead trees.'

'It's not like that. I promise.'

'Fine.'

They went out the back, locking up, and went down the garden to the hedge. John began to climb through.

'Jesus Christ, John...'

'It's just this bit, I promise...'

'This is not what I had in mind.'

With a hand on his arm, she scrambled through. On the other side, he stopped to let her admire the woods.

'Beautiful, isn't it?'

'It's just trees, John.'

'It's nature. Something we never had in New York.'

'Central Park is nature.'

'It's not the same thing.'

'How?' She pushed his arm away to walk alone.

'There are deer here. And hares. And other things you would never see in New York. Birds, maybe eagles. I dunno.'

The day was cold and the floor of the forest glistened from a morning downpour. The smell of wet foliage filled the air. The dampness and heaviness of incoming winter. The air laden with moisture and the heavy odor of marsh. Wet fern. Above them, a bird called.

'What was that?'

'A bird.'

'Like no bird I ever heard.'

'That's what I'm talking about,' he said. 'Nature.'

She rested a hand on his arm as they stepped over a puddle, taking it away again as they ventured onto the path.

'See? Just like I told you. And this is our back garden now.'

She looked out through the trees. Out there somewhere, the whisper of a brook. She wrinkled her nose. The smell was not pleasing to her. It didn't agree. She pulled the neck of her sweater up around her face.

'Are you cold?'

'No, John, I'm not cold.'

'Don't be like that. I'm only concerned about you.'

'I'm fine.'

'Wanna talk about last night?'

She closed her eyes momentarily. 'It was just a bad dream.'

'Seemed pretty bad. I've never seen you like that before.'

'I'd rather not talk about it.'

'Fine. We don't have to.'

They heard a distressed squeal from somewhere out in the trees. They both froze. Her hand found his arm.

'What the fuck is that, John?'

'What? I dunno, an animal of some kind.'

'John it sounds like a baby.'

'It's not a baby.'

'It sounds like a fucking baby, John.'

'Jesus Christ, will you relax? It's not a baby.'

They took a step toward the noise and stopped. She looked at him. 'We have to go see.'

'Why don't you stay here and I'll go have a look.'

'John, for fuck's sake, I'm not ten years old.'

'Why are you swearing at me? I'm not swearing...'

She shook her head and looked away. 'Would you just lead the way please.'

He looked at her in incomprehension, then set off into the trees. She followed. About thirty meters out beyond the path, they found a trap with a young jackrabbit in it.

'For fuck's sake,' she whispered through her teeth. 'Who does such a thing?'

'I dunno. Hunters?'

'Of course it's hunters, John. I mean, it's only young. Look at it.'

'I know. I see it.'

'Well, don't just stand there. Let it out.'

He held up his hands. 'It's not our trap, honey. I can't just let it go.'

'John, it's a suffering animal. You can't leave it here like this.'

Above, they heard the same bird call.

'You hear that? Whatever that is up there, it's gonna kill it if you don't let it go. So please, would you just free it so we can go home. I've had enough of nature already.'

'Fine.' He shook his head and knelt by the trap. 'I'll free it.'

He looked at the tiny animal for a minute. Helpless, terrified. Struggling to free itself and only tightening the snare around its neck. John tried to grab it and the thing tugged away, squealing.

'What are you doing, John?'

'I'm trying to get hold of it. In a humane way.'

'Humane. Oh thank God for that.'

He glared up at her. 'Could you not make this any more

difficult than it already is?'

She turned away. He got hold of the rabbit around the body and pushed it against the ground, and struggled to release the snare around it.

'Anytime today, John.'

'I'm trying...'

'Try harder. I'm getting cold.'

He cursed under his breath. The rabbit's cries were painful to him. He gritted his teeth. Katie lifted her hands to her ears but it did no good.

'John...'

'I'm trying goddamnit, I'm trying.'

'I swear, John...'

'Look, I can't get the damned thing loose, okay.'

'Then you're gonna have to kill it.'

'Kill it?'

'Yes! You're the goddamned outdoors man, aren't you? Chopping wood and what else. Just kill it.'

'It's a living animal, honey.'

'Stop calling me *honey*, will you? Do something, for Christ's sake, just make it stop screaming.'

She was shouting now. He looked up at her, perplexed. 'Just give me a min—'

'Just kill the fucking thing!'

He picked up a rock and smashed it in the head. He turned his hand over as he stood up, his fingers spattered with the creature's blood.

'There, you happy. I fucking killed it.'

She turned and walked away. He fought the urge to vomit.

She went to bed. Unable to take the cold silence of the house, he went outside and got the ladder from the shed. He took it out front and put it against the wall of the house, climbed up and began to scrape out the guttering. He felt better. Outside was more pleasant than inside.

He was cleaning the chicken wire that protected the

downspout when he heard a shout from the lane and turned.

A man waved from the gate.

'How are ya?'

'Good.' He waved back. 'Let me come down from here.'

He descended the ladder and walked up to the gate and stretched his hand across it. The man took his hand and shook.

'Good to meet you at last,' he said. 'We all been mighty curious about our new neighbors.'

'Oh yeah?'

'You know how people are. It's the wife, mostly. The women like to talk, don't they?' He adjusted the tip of his cap, either by way of apology or to elicit agreement.

'Yeah, I guess I'd be too. I'm John.'

'Martin. Marty, you can call me.'

'Nice to meet you Marty. You next door?'

He pointed up the street. 'Two doors up. Next door, that's the Levens. They come in May and leave in September. Year round, it's only ourselves, Gina and Earl, and the Clellands.' He pointed to a series of houses up and down the street. 'So you guys are gonna be full-timers?'

John nodded. 'We hope so. We've moved everything down here and we don't particularly wanna move back.'

'New York or Boston?'

'New York.'

'Uh-huh.' He nodded and turned to look up the street. He turned back to John. 'Good solid house you've bought there. The wife wanted to buy it a couple of years back before Elliot picked it up. She just loves the look of it, with the dormers, you know. We wanted to do it to our own, years back, but we got bats under our roof. Can't move the damn things because they're protected. But yeah, that's a nice little house you got there.'

'We like it. Katie's been dreaming of it for some years now.'

'Katie's the wife?'

'Yep.' John tilted his head toward the house. 'Sleeping. We've a baby on the way. Due over winter.'

'God bless you.' Marty squinted.

'Yeah. Thanks.'

'Fine thing, bringing a child into this world.'

'So we've been told.'

'Well, I wish you both the best. And give my regards to your good wife.' He held out his hand and they shook. 'And if you ever need anything...'

'Thank you.'

'You be well. And don't be strangers.'

'See you, Marty.'

The man went off up the road and John watched him go. Marty turned once to look back. John waved, then went back to the ladder. He picked it up and carried it around the back of the house and leaned it against the wall over the glass doors of the kitchen and climbed.

About halfway down the gutter he put his hands to something solid. His stomach tightened. He knew. He took out his hand and opened it, seeing in his palm a small carved eagle. Dirty and discolored but he could make it out well. The urge came on him to throw it. Somehow, he knew it would be futile. He was pushing it into the top pocket of his shirt when he slipped and took a spill to the concrete below and hit the ground with a sickening thud.

SEVEN

THE STREET was dusty and the air forlorn. The log-built cabins with their thatched roofs and small windows hid a fearful people; the children were corralled into those cramped indoor spaces, beyond the walls of the huts and outside the perimeter the vast perturbing expanse of a hostile land, bountiful yet filled with execration and woe. Beyond the fences that surrounded their precarious homestead, none ventured lightly. Beyond was a land soaked in blood, a land with an unquenchable thirst for it. And there were those too whose hunger and thirst for it were not to be slaked.

The man in the thick black coat wiped the crud from his mouth with the back of a dirty hand. He proceeded up the dusty street in the dark. A head in a doorway nodded at his passing. Out beyond the fence he heard a bloody cry. He gritted his teeth.

At the end of the dusty street he stopped outside the long house. He spat, wiping his mouth once more before opening the door and stepping inside.

The voice of the minister boomed. The man slipped along the back wall, pausing and looking around him. A few familiar faces caught his eye. He nodded. Licked his lips. Cleared the corners of his lips with a thumb and forefinger. He turned to look at the minister.

—And what of our hardships here, my brethren? Have we

not, do we not, suffer dailie on account of these wicked and barbarous creatures? And in coming here to this fatal land, our chiefest food hath been hope and tears our chiefest drinke. Is it not so? God himself is witnesse to our suff'ring on this account. I came here with the first of ye, and seen many a good soul perish, and put the same in the ground and did give them a Christian burial here in this heathen land, far from the bosom of the mother countrie. For here yet hath we to sanctify this soil, tread underfoot by Lucifer himself since time immemorial. The devill is afoot, yes! Abroad, beyond—hear him now outside these very walls? Put your ear to the door and hear him crie for Christian bloud. He shrieks like a harpie, cries for the souls of the innocent believers. Did he not, only a few days ago, carrie off two of our very own maids? And what suff'ring must they be enduring at this moment, I ask ye? What iniquities are these beasts, these Sodomites, inflicting on our good Christian virgins?

The man in black licked his lips and the corners of his lips but a hellish dryness was upon him.

—These savage beasts have carried our good and pure virgins into captivity, into temptation and concupiscence and carnalitie, and God forgive us all, but may at this very moment be raping and polluting our very own daughters...

Those present growled and gnashed their teeth. One man stamped the earth beneath his feet like a goat.

—Foul is the way of these animals, bestial their manner and way of life. Licentiousness, we've seen it with some of our very own. These native women like serpents have slithered into the beds of some of our men—husbands, *Christians*—these snakes opened their legs and tempted and corrupted and put to the devill even the best and devoutest among us...

The man in black sunk his head into his shoulders.

—These are not creatures of God. They are not beholden to God's holie church. Recall Ham, son of Noah, who provoked the wrath of the Almighty by gazing upon the nakedness of his drunken father. Driven into exile, his people were compelled to wander the dry earth endlessly in their heathen ways, the condemned and despised of God. Well brethren, I say to thee—here, all around us their impure and defiled women, even in the beds of some amongst us—this is the land into which we have stumbled! Yes! Here we have arrived, among the very descendants of Ham. Hear them cry and cavort outside these very walls? That is not the cry of a poor and innocent savage—that is the devill's consort, come against the church of Christ in unholie warre! Yet here we are, and here we have been sent. It is our own beloved father in heaven that has sent us forth into the land of the infidell. And why may not Christians have libertie to go forth among them in their wastelands and woods as lawfully as Abraham did go among the Sodomites? For the worshippe these heathens confess to is no diff'rent from the worshippe of Baal. Reports we have and true of their own pawwwaws stamping the earth and calling up the devill in his sicknesse, and have ye not seen it yourselves, men of God, their warriors by the riverside, dancing and attempting to summon Lucifer to put the English boats to flyte? Are they not cruell and ungodly? Who but Lucifer dwells in the soul of a beast whose food is the flesh of man, who with teeth like dogges doth pursue us with ravenous appetite to eat of our flesh and devoure us? Satan himself wills the doings of these dark-skinned brutes, and were it not for the will of the Lord then all our daughters would be chained to the heathen bed and violated in the darkest of manners...

—Vile! Vile!

—Vile, yes. Vile and debased are the devill's creatures. Look into the trees—there they dwell, waiting for us to turn our backs. Well, we shall not turn our backs...

—No!

—No, brethren, we shall not turn our backs on the devill. For in a prison we be, yet do we have Christ, and better a prison with Christ than libertie without him. And yet in a furnace we live, better a furnace with the presence of Christ than in a kinglie palace without. For how sweet is thy word, Lord, sweeter than the honey and the honey combe. And we pray that our Lord give strength and guidance to our young daughters under the heathen yoke that he may keep them to his bosom that they may not suffer violation at heathen hands. For our young daughters are being tested, as are we. Did Christ himself not carrie the word among the heathens, and did not his message fall on deaf ears? And what was the Lord's response to the rejection of Christ by the unbelievers? He struck down the tempell and cleaved it in two!

—Lord hear us!

Yes brethren, the sons of Christ shall not suffer their daughters to be kidnapped and violated, and the beds of our menfolk to be inhabited by snakes. Brethren, though we live in hope yet drown dailie in our tears, we are children of God who live and dwell in Christ, and through the mercie of the Lord shall the devill and his lying pawwaws be confounded. The hands of the heathen reake with the bloud of my countrymen, they have murthered and massacred and slit the throats of God-fearing folk and desecrated their very bodies, yet I tell you today, that God will putteth away the ungodly like a drosse, for it is God's ordinance to put a curse upon them and kill them as the children of Israel did Baalam...

—Hear hear!

The man in black chewed his lip, his fists balled and fit for killing and his eyes bloodshot.

—For God is above us, and God laughs at his enemies and the enemies of his people, and if we yet live in the fierie oven, it is they that shall perish in it and burn in the flames of the hellfire. Thus the Lord will judge the heathen and fill the land with dead.

—As the Lord is my witness!

The room reeked with the thirst for blood.

—It is your duty to execute those whom God our righteous judge hath condemned for sloth, self-indulgence, deceit, rape, devill worship and concupiscence, and for blaspheming his sacred majestie and murthering his servants. Brethren, go forth and execute vengeance upon the heathen, binde his king in chaines and their nobles in fetters of iron, and make their multitudes fall under your warlike weapons. Set them to the ground and put your feet on their proud necks, and consecrate the earth with their heathen blood.

—Murtherers!

—Apostates!

—Sodomites!

Alive in the hunger for blood and fire, they screamed as one. The man in black would soon slake his thirst.

EIGHT

John? Can you hear me, John?

He came around. His wife was beside him, staring at him wide-eyed and afraid.

'Oh Jesus, John... thank God.'

She was weeping. She shook her head and pressed her forehead to his hand. He raised it feebly to run it over her hair.

'How long...?'

'You've been here for three hours.'

'Jesus.'

'You scared the shit out of me, John.'

'I'm sorry.'

She shook her head. 'Don't say sorry. It was an accident. Just promise me it won't happen again.'

He sat up and groaned. He raised his hand to his head.

'What did the doctor say?'

'Bruised ribs. None broken. Concussion. You broke your little finger though.'

He looked down at his hand in bandage. 'For fuck's sake.'

'No more chopping wood, huh?'

'I'm sure I could manage with one hand.'

'Just leave it be, would you John?'

'I'm a little bit bruised but I'm not an invalid, Katie.'

She heard someone come in and turned her head. 'Well if you

won't listen to me, maybe you'll listen to him.'

The doctor approached the bed. 'Mr Mears. How are you feeling?'

He grimaced. 'A little knocked about?'

'I bet. That was quite a spill you took. Look, I see no reason to keep you here. I'm gonna let your wife take you home, but I'm sure it goes without saying, you need to rest up and take it easy for a few days. No climbing ladders, no cleaning gutters—'

'No chopping wood.' Katie glared at him.

'No chopping wood. Do yourself a favor and listen to your wife. I've given her the rundown. I know it's not ideal—she's heavily pregnant—but let her look after you for a few days. As far as she's able.'

'I'm sure that won't be necessary, Doctor.'

'Oh yes it will. Do as she says.'

'Yes, Doctor.'

'Good. I'll sign your discharge and ask your wife to come with me for a moment. We'll be right back.'

Katie squeezed his hand and stood up. 'I'll be right back.'

They left the ward. John looked around. There were two beds in the room but he was alone. He looked out the window at the gray sky and closed his eyes. Then he turned to the chair next to the bed where his clothes sat in a basket. He sat up, clenching his teeth and hissing.

'*Fuck...*'

Clutching his side with his bandaged hand, he put his legs over the edge of the bed and slid until his feet hit the floor. He stood. Peeling the gown over his head with one hand, he dropped it on the bed and looked at his side which was a deep blue and purple from under his arm to his lower rib. He winced.

Lifting his pants, his slipped into them using one hand, first one leg then the other. He struggled to button them and fix his belt, then he put on his shirt and socks. When he was attired, he sat. He felt it in his pocket pressing against his thigh. He put his hand in and pulled out the carved white eagle. He felt a cold shudder, like someone had just opened a tap and the heat had drained from him in a rush. Strange flashes beset his muddled mind: an unsettling man in the woods, an Indian in native attire watching him from the treeline. A dream?

Katie came back through the doors and he shoved it into his pocket.

'Jesus, John—could you not have waited for me to help you? Why are you always so pigheaded?'

'I can still dress myself, Katie. Don't be freaking out. It's almost as if you want to mother me.'

She glared at him. 'What's that supposed to mean?'

'Nothing. Come on—help me get my coat on.'

'Here, sit down. I'll get you a coffee.'

She sat him on the sofa and went to the kitchen and made coffee.

'I'll set the fire.'

'You don't have to do that, Katie.'

'I don't mind.'

'I would prefer you didn't.'

She took a deep breath. 'Like you said, I'm not an invalid.'

'Okay.'

She went out of the room and into the kitchen.

'Please don't carry too much,' he shouted after her.

She came back and built the fire and lit it, and went and made coffee, and sat down with him on the sofa. They sat cradling their cups and watching the flames of the fire. John's eyes drooped pleasantly. He felt a strange commingling with the cuspate scintillation of the flame, the fire an incongruity, extratemporal, a thing that existed in the mind more profoundly than it did between those four walls or in any hearth, and in that it was an egress to something beyond. His wife's hand on his thigh prevented his departure.

'Are you alright?'

He put his hand on hers. 'Yeah, I'm good.'

'Quite a day, huh?'

'Yeah.' His eyes opened and closed slowly. 'What time is it?'

'Almost eight.'

'Is it too early for bed?'

'After the day we've had? I'd say not. But aren't you hungry?'

'More tired. What do you say we have an early night?'

She patted his knee. 'Sure.'

She put down her cup and got up and put the guard over the hearth, and they went upstairs together. She helped him change into pajamas and she got undressed and into her nightie, and together they slipped into bed and fell asleep even with the curtains undrawn.

Downstairs, though they couldn't hear it, the fire smoldered and crackled.

In fires after dark things remain alive, and things that have long since died come back to visit. They come in from the cold, from the empty deserts and the woods, and the swamps and the lonely coasts, and in the fire they rediscover points lost in time, moments, and also things they lost or were taken from them, often in blood and rage. Thus is the fire a place of assembly and gathering and the locus of past griefs, their begetting and their resolution.

Into such a night by such a fire came again the man with the melting face. Found himself staring into the flame, from what place or from what time he did not care to recall, for called back to the flame he found himself gathered, like all souls rent apart by loss and suffering and grief who cannot part this earth accordingly, drawn back to the fire for the retribution of past evils. He held his hand out to the flame, felt its heat and its power, and in it knew and understood the reality of who he was and why he was here. He closed his eyes and prayed to whom and in whatever way was his custom, then he bowed to the fire and stood up. He climbed the stairs.

In the room, at the foot of the bed, he stood and watched her. Saw the bump of her swollen belly, a child within. He too had had a child. Had several. Had a wife. A beautiful wife. Woke with her beside him every day, saw his children, saw them born and saw them grow, and then... then came fire and blood.

Came now he, one forged in fire and blood, his face ash and clay. He climbed onto the bed and over her sleeping body. Perched over her, he smelled the fledgling life within her. He leaned in until he felt her breath on his face. That's when she opened her eyes. The whites of her eyes, pupils dilated. He looked into her, saw the frozen terror. Smelled it. He leaned in so that she felt the clammy wetness of his skin on hers. She tried to scream but only whimpered. He licked her face to see how her fear tasted. It tasted metallic. He looked in her eyes. She beheld his face, the dripping chiaroscuro of his timeless visage. She tried to call, scream her husband's name—*john!*—but her throat was stone. The man pulled back the covers and ran his hand over her belly, then leaned in and sniffed. He could smell the young, hear its beating heart—*john, help me*—lifted her nightie to expose her swollen midriff, scraped his nails over her skin—*help me john, jesus christ help*—his clammy hands on her belly, his lips at her bellybutton, she frozen, the weight of a man on her chest holding her down, clawing creeping terror that death was only moments away—*john would you fucking wake up, wake up john!*—He parted her legs. Put his cold hand to her sex. Put two cold damp fingers inside her and pushed up into her—*for the love of god john hes trying to kill me, hes going to kill our baby*—his fingers reaching, pushing, she feels his fingers grasping for the child within her, tears streaming down her immobile face, not only the fear now but the rage in her too—*he wants to kill our baby john, would you fucking wake up, wake the fuck up!*—his fingers like the branches of an evil weed reaching up into her insides—

She screamed.

NINE

Gaunt and drawn, she sat on the sofa. He paced the floor in front of the cold spent fire. There had been little sleep, and what sleep there had been was tormented and fearful. For all it was, the night had left them worn and defeated.

'We need to get out of here, John. Something is wrong with this house, this... *place*.'

'Honey, there's nothing wrong with this place. You had a couple of bad dreams is all. It's probably perfectly normal when people move. It's a massive upheaval. It's stressful. Things get craz—'

'This is not just some bad dreams, John—I had a man on top of me in my sleep. He had his fingers inside me, for fuck's sake. I felt him *inside* me...'

He stopped in front of her and fell to his knees. 'Baby, we've come so far, let's not throw it all away after only a month. Please give this a chance. We've worked so hard, for us, for our new child—'

'John, it's our child I'm worried about, don't you see? I think our child is in danger—'

'Jesus, Katie —'

'Don't patronize me, John. I know what I felt. And I know it sounds crazy, but for the love of God, believe me—it was a man on top of me and he put his hands into me. I know what I felt, and I swear, I *swear*, it has something to do with this house...'

He shook his head. 'Baby, I promise you this house is safe. The doors are locked, I double-checked them, there's been no break-in, I checked all the windows. I swear, we're in no danger here.'

'Jesus fucking Christ, would you listen to me John? I'm not saying there was someone in the house, but maybe a, I dunno, a *presence* or something. I know it. I *felt* it. Will you please just believe me?'

'Do you know how crazy that sounds? I mean, can you hear yourself right now?'

She shook her head. 'It's not just me, John. It's you too. What about that day I came in and found you staring into the fire, huh—what was that? And what about your fall? I've never seen you fall in my life. I mean, you used to work in construction. Are you gonna tell me you haven't sensed something weird about this place?'

'No, Katie. I haven't.' He stood up and went out to the kitchen.

'Where are you going?'

When he came back, he had a bottle of pills in his hand and a glass of water. She began to weep.

'Jesus Christ, what are you gonna do—drug me to keep me here? Won't you listen to me, won't you? I wanna leave here, John. I wanna go back to my mom's. I don't like it here, listen to me, *please...*'

'These are baby-friendly, I promise. It's just to help you relax, just for a few hours...'

'No, John, please...'

'Do it for me, sweetheart. I'm begging you.'

'John, no...' He raised the pill to her mouth. She shook her head. 'Please...'

He placed it in her mouth and handed her the glass. 'Do it for me, I'm begging you...'

She shook her head, her face wet with tears, as he raised the glass to her mouth.

Later that afternoon after she'd woken up and after they'd eaten, he told her to put on her coat.

'What? Why? I'm very tired. Let's not go out, please.'

'We're only going down the street Katie. Some of the neighbors have invited us over for coffee. I thought it'd be good for us to, you know, help settle in.'

'Aww John, you arranged to go out? I wished you'd have told me.'

'It just happened, while you were sleeping. Come on. I want you to see this is a nice place and there's nothing at all scary about it.'

She sighed. Too tired and too spent, she acquiesced. 'Fine.'

They put on their coats and went out, and walked down the lane to a small cottage two doors down. Single story like their own, it was older in style, saltbox and with the walls shingled.

They stepped inside the picket gate, John closing it behind them, and before they'd made it to the top of the path, the door opened. A woman smiled, a man appearing at her shoulder.

'Hey folks,' John said.

'Hey there. Come on up.'

They stopped at the door. 'Marty, Sarah, this is my wife Katie. Katie, this is Marty and Sarah.'

'A pleasure to meet you, sweetheart. We were so worried to hear you've been having a bad time of it...' Katie glared at John but said nothing. 'Well, don't just stand there. Come in out of the cold.'

They stepped inside and Marty took their coats, and Sarah led them to the sitting room.

'Here, sit yourselves down. Marty's just gone to get coffee. So, how are y'all?'

'We're fine,' Katie said. 'Just fine.'

'How's that baby coming along?'

'Oh, he's kicking. Gonna be a little footballer by the looks of it.'

'That's just great. You found yourself a doctor down here?'

Katie nodded. 'Yep. We found someone over at Lawrence

Memorial in New London who we're both very happy with. We were there for a check a few days ago. And yesterday, for him...' She pointed at John.

'He told us about the fall.' Sarah shook her head. 'Terrible thing...'

Marty came back in the room with a tray and put it down. 'Here you go, folks. These are my wife's very own cookies.' He looked at Katie. 'You can eat cookies, can't ya?'

Katie smiled and nodded. 'Yes.'

'Good. Then tuck in.'

'We were just talking about John's fall.'

'Oh yeah? Gotta be careful, especially with the wife pregnant and all. Hey if you want the number of a guy who'll come out and clean your guttering for ya, just you say. I know a guy, great handyman. I used to do everything myself, but now she won't let me get up a ladder no more.'

Sarah shook her head. 'You'd end up in the hospital like John here, you old fool.'

Marty waved his hand dismissively. 'Not a goddamned thing wrong with me.'

Sarah turned to Katie. 'So, when you expecting?'

'End of February.'

'Couldn't wait to spring proper, huh?' Sarah laughed. 'Ah well, they come when they come.'

'You got kids of your own?'

She nodded. 'Two. Both up in Boston. We got two grandkids too. Amazing how quickly they grow up.'

'I bet.'

They fell silent and sipped their coffee, and sat with the stoicism of people in new company.

'So you're having a little boy?' Sarah said.

'Yeah, a boy. We're both delighted.'

'Got a name for him yet?'

Katie glanced at John. 'We're keeping it close to our chest. You know...'

'Sure. Well, I can tell you, around here sure is a great place to raise a kid—good schools, lots of open space. You sure picked a good spot.'

There was another moment of silence as Katie cradled her cup nervously and glanced at her husband. John cleared his throat.

'Well, that's the thing you see, Katie's been having some trouble settling in. The place doesn't seem to be sitting with her right.'

She shook her head. 'Like John says, it's probably nothing. I just... I've been having these—'

'Aww, sweetheart—I know exactly what you mean. When we first moved down here, it was a full year before I could sleep right—'

'My God, dear—don't be telling her that,' Marty said.

'But you know what I mean, it's the different air, the sounds, the atmosphere. It all takes getting used to.'

'Well actually, Sarah, it's more than that. I've been having these visions—'

'More like *dreams*, honey. Right?'

She didn't look at him. '...These dreams, I dunno what they are, and they're terrifying, really, so lifelike and frightening—'

'Oh my...'

'Well, *twice*. Not a whole bunch of times. Right honey?'

'Remember how I got the nightmares during my first pregnancy, dear?'

'Oh yeah...' Marty shook his head thoughtfully.

'My God, it was terrible. I didn't know what I was waking up to...'

'I dunno,' Katie said, 'but it feels to me like it's connected to the house somehow—'

John laughed nervously. 'I told her she's crazy. I mean, it's crazy, right?'

This time she threw him a look. 'It's just, something doesn't *feel* right...'

'Oh sweetheart. Well, if you're worried something happened in that house, like somebody was murdered or something—'

'Jesus, Sarah...'

'Language, Martin Bartlett. If you're worried about something like that, then don't be. Marjorie and Elliot lived there for years before moving up to Providence, and before that it was the Underhills, and to my mind there was nothing untoward happened there. He didn't even die in the house, Underhill, did he Marty? He was with his son in New London when he passed...'

Marty shook his head. 'Need we be so morbid? We've just met these good folk.'

'But Marty, she's worried the house is possessed or something.'

'No, it's not that, really. It's just, something doesn't *feel right.*'

Sarah waved a hand. 'Don't you worry. There's nothing wrong with that there house. Why I wanted to buy it myself a few years back, didn't I Marty?'

'Sure did.'

'I'm sure we'll grow into it,' John said. 'Right honey?'

She didn't reply, just looked into her coffee cup.

'You know what you need, sweetheart? A cookie. Here—try one of these. I promise you, once you've had a bite, you'll feel a whole lot better...'

John opened the shed door and stepped inside, turned on the light. Closed the door behind him. He reached up to the top shelf, pushed aside the tin of paint and took down the idols. He set them on the worktop in front of him: the jackrabbit, the fawn, the eagle. He put his hand in his pocket and pulled out another: a man's head, carved in the same fashion. It fit snugly in the palm of his hand. He'd found it nestled in a miniature basket of potpourri in their neighbor's bathroom, and finding it there knew it was meant for him. He'd pocketed it without a thought. Now here it was, an addition to his collection. He set them side by side on the worktop. It was a meeting, a convergence. A summoning. He knew not the import but was sure he would come to understand, come to know the wherefore of his being here. The weight of history was upon his shoulders but he knew it not. He left the idols out, for he sensed they would soon be complete, and then whatever awaited their reunion would show itself and make its purpose known.

When he went outside, Katie was sitting at the table under the outdoor heating wrapped in her coat. She looked at him coldly.

He sat down.

'What are you doing in there?'

'Sharpening the ax. Why?'

She looked away.

'Are you alright?'

She was quiet for a moment before speaking. 'Not really, John. No. I can't believe you dragged me over there to let them sell me on this place.'

'That's not what I was doing, Katie. I just wanted them to reassure you that there's nothing weird or strange about the house.'

'My point exactly. To sell it to me. And why did you keep undermining what I was saying?'

'I don't understand what you mean...'

'I mean, "I told her she's crazy. That's crazy, right"? What was that? Do you think I'm crazy?'

'I don't think you're crazy honey, no.'

'Don't fucking "honey" me.'

'I really don't know what you're talking about, Katie. I don't know what to say...'

'Then don't say anything.' She drank from the cup nestled in her lap. 'I've made a decision, John. I'm calling Donnie tomorrow and asking him to come pick me up and take me to Mom's. I'm packing a bag and I'm leaving. I can't stay here while I'm pregnant. I don't even know if I can come back here in spring. You wanna stay, you stay. It's up to you. But I'm going. Something bad's gonna happen if I stay here, I can feel it.'

'Katie—'

'Don't say it. Don't say a word. I've made up my mind and

nothing you say will change it.'

He said nothing.

Came he in the night, for he sensed the change. Came he from amidst the fire, he born of fire and blood. Blood begets blood and such debt is eternal, and the blood of children is a debt unforgivable. Came he with the weight of history, and the anguish of his people and the terrible weight of a continent behind him, a continent birthed in his people's slaughter, his hands soaked in his children's blood. Came he for vengeance.

His feet ashen, came he up the stairs, the dark footprints on the floor underfoot. Into the bedroom. By the bed. He looked at her sleeping there, her swollen belly rising and falling with the beat of her weak and petrified heart. Yes, the time had come.

He turned to the man, pulled back the covers, lifted his arm and placed the thing into his hand and closed the palm.

John awoke from sleep and opened his eyes. The room was quiet. He'd felt a presence. He looked down at his hand, raised it to his face and opened it. In his hand, the final idol: a sleeping serpent. Yet now was the time for its awakening. He sensed its coming.

Hobomok. Come for his debt.

TEN

THE MAN in the black coat led his band of mercenaries through the woods in the dead of night, with them a contingent of savage. The men were tired and hungry, bitterness and rage their only sustenance these past two days. Their tracker had assured them they'd be at the village in the dead of night when darkness would give them cover; now dawn was fast approaching and the village was still not in sight. The man in black was ready for killing the savage.

—We stop here, the chief of the injuns said.

The man in black raised his musket at the chief's head. —If you or your men stop for even a second I'll shoot you all where you stand. Keep moving.

He turned to the tracker, taking the knife from his belt and pointing it at him. —How far?

The tracker pointed an indeterminate direction into the woods. —Here.

Twenty minutes later they set eyes on it. An encampment on a hilltop with fortress fencing, a few wisps of smoke rising from within. The sunrise was upon them.

—We move on it now, he said.

—Sir, better we wait for night. We can camp here for the day and take them at nightfall.

—We go now.

Tired and worn yet rage drove them on.

The sun was coming over the horizon when they gathered just beyond the fort. They kneeled in prayer and exhorted God that they might bring the bestial savage under the boot and vanquish the blood of their countrymen, and when they'd raised their prayers to heaven they took up position at both entrances of the fort. The savages circled the entrances to prevent escape, the two captains led a handful of men inside.

The first that were roused from their beds were run through with the sword. Cries announced the arrival of the Englishmen: —Owanux! Owanux! and the injuns in their confusion did scatter wildly. The man in black entered a hut where they'd awoken to the shouts, and he run his sword through the breast of the mother and beheaded the two young daughters. He spat, rushing outside to take on the warriors, these brutes who fought in all their shameless nakedness. Cutting one in the stomach he watched his guts spill out and almost slipped in them. Around them they fell, even some of his own, and the natives shot him with their arrows but his thick ox-hide coat kept the arrows from his body. They must have thought him a god. He cut down a running woman, cleaving her from neck to belly. Behind him one of his men cut down a warrior and sliced off his genitals stuffing them into the dying man's mouth. The man in black retreated to the entrance where one of the allied savages was waiting with a firebrand, and taking it he began to set the huts on fire, those with the dead inside and even the living. They ran in havoc through the village, some on fire and some cut through, one woman with a knife still in her eye socket and still clutching a baby to her breast, and a man pulling himself over the ground, one of his legs cleaved off above the knee, and now the reek of burning flesh filling their noses, so much so that even the savages beyond the walls retched. Children too, cut down and dismembered and beheaded, babies thrown into the fire, —God shall bring down hell upon the devill's beasts! they screamed, Put the foul savage to the slaughter! Inside a hut, a sword was driven up inside a woman's sex in front of her children, the children then put to the knife. Outside, their menfolk burned, so many that the blood that ran from them quenched the fires that tore through the village. And when those that made it past the blade did flee the ring of fire, they were cut down with musket fire by the men who lay in wait in the trees, and if they did make it past the muskets they were slain by the allied savages. One of the Englishmen put his lance through a mother holding a babe in her arms, the woman falling and the babe impaled on the blade still, with which he continued to slay the natives. Mothers, their bellies cut open, children sliced up and dismembered, and when it was done and nothing but the smoking reeking ruins of the village remained, the retreating Englishmen kicked the heads of the natives downhill like footballs. They came upon one man in the woods, injured and not far from death, and they impaled him on a spike and put him over a fire. —Burn the devill out of him! they cried. For there was no salvation for those who feasted on the flesh of men and were the violators of God's daughters. When his body was sufficiently charred they took him down and scraped his skin from his body with oyster shells, the man with a breath still in him. Then they dragged the last of the living children down to the shore to be sold off as chattel.

—Trulie we have done God's work today, gentlemen.

—And all that even before breakfast.

ELEVEN

ASHEN HANDS pulled back the sheets, exposing her sleeping form. The baby inside her, the child's heart beating. He could hear it, faint and indistinct, but there all the same beneath the resonance of the mother's heart. Two hearts in unison. Smelled it too, the baby. He pushed up her nightdress to reveal the swollen belly, inside a whole world yet unraveled, a story that would remain untold. She was asleep. The pills had seen to that. The mother. The mother eternal. The mother who was and would always be, no matter the place nor the time, the mother and child a thing immemorial. And yet one may die yet another live. Strange, the turning of the world and its direction, and the taking and the ending of life not at the sole discretion of God, yet also at man's. And when one man make it his province, so does it become that of all men. The life that is taken will yet be repaid.

He spread her legs and ripped her underwear to reveal her sex, entrance to the womb and the font of all life. He went to the wardrobe and took out a coat hanger, and unraveling the metal returned to the bed, clambering again on top of her. He fed the pointed end of it into her sex and up inside her. Feeling the foreign body invade her, she opened her eyes. Come again he, the man with the melting face. He looked into her eyes and grinned. She tried to move but couldn't, the weight of a blood-soaked continent pinning her to the bed. She tried to shake her head, to plead with her eyes, to beg for the life of her unborn child. She felt the jagged tip of the metal tear the walls of her vagina, felt the blood trickle from her, felt it rip her cervix and tear the wall of her uterus, the waters breaking and spilling from her—*no, god no, stop*—the baby struggling as the steel pierced its tiny unformed skull—*dont kill my baby*—the baby inside her screaming silently in the womb—*my baby*—the man with the melting face feeling the life drain from the mother's womb—*god no, don't do this*—the blood from her staining the white sheets of the bed, and the amniotic fluid, the aqua vitae, no longer life-giving, flood out, the life ending—*my child, my babyyyy*—a few sharp pokes to make sure—*youre killing my fucking baby*—the silent screams from the mother of a child that will never live. When it is done he pulls out the metal. Her face wet, her eyes tortured, her body screaming too as he pushes two fingers in her, and then a hand, her fingers clawing the sheets of the bed, the only parts of her body that move, his hand, then the arm, reaching, reaching up inside her until the hand is around the dead child in her womb—*john*—she screams but he does not hear, and the baby is ripped from her womb, pulled out of her and held before her.

    —john, kill me john—

TWELVE

*—Your baby's gone, sir. It's... gone. —I don't understand what you
mean. What do you mean, doctor? Gone? —I don't know what to tell
you, Mr Mears. She's lost the child. (shouting now)—What do you
mean, lost? Talk sense to me please, how can a woman just lose a baby?
—Mr Mears, please calm down... —I am fucking calm. My wife is
in critical condition... —Sir...*

IT WAS MANY DAYS before she opened her eyes. And when she
did she registered only the bright lights of the hospital, not
the face of the nurse, not even the face of her husband that sat
beside her clutching her damp hand. He called for Dr. Chaudri
and she came, and shone a light in her eyes and reported with
considerable worry that she seemed to be in a state of catatonia,
but not to worry, she was sure she would soon recover.

'There's the other issue that we should talk about, Mr.
Mears...'

'Which is?'

'The, you know, appalling trauma to her vaginal area...'

The police came. They questioned him. He told them he'd
taken sleeping pills and had no recollection of the night.

'Nothing?'

'Nothing.'

He took them to the house and they searched the house and

examined the bedroom and took samples.

'No sign of breaking or entering,' they said.

'I was led to believe it wasn't the kind of thing that happens here,' he said.

They left. They would talk again very soon, they told him.

On the third day, she made eye contact with him. In her eyes was a terror that would never leave her. They upped her medication.

'Can I take her home, Doctor?' he asked.

'That's not a good idea,' she said.

'She might come around quicker in our own home.'

'She's not leaving here until her wounds have healed.'

'Doctor—'

'I'm not discussing it with you. And by the way, why aren't her family here?'

'I'm talking to them every day. There's some stuff going on.' She nodded.

On the thirteenth day she was released from hospital and he took her home and put her in bed. He gave her her pills and laid her head on the pillow.

'Don't try to move. I'm gonna do everything for you,' he said.

She closed her eyes and drifted off.

She came around. He was there next to her. 'Let me out of here,' she croaked. 'Let me go...'

'I got you,' he said. He mopped her forehead with a cool damp cloth.

Days, nights. Sun coming in the curtains, the darkness of deep night. His snoring form beside her. She immobile in the bed. Weeping. Sleep. Night terrors. The man with the melting face in her dreams. Her nightmares. Her dead baby that would never be. Her life, over. The man beside her...

One night she awoke, the house filled with a vile odor that filled her with horror.

In pain, and afraid, she put her legs over the edge of the

bed. She crossed the floor to the top of the stairs. Hesitatingly, she descended. The house was filled with a choking smoke. She followed it to the kitchen where she found the door to the cupboard open and the trapdoor agape. She choked back a cough and peered inside, saw the light of a fire within.

'John?'

No answer. She wet a towel and put it to her face and climbed down in her white nightie, a ghost of a woman. Down below the fire burned, in the corner in the hole in the floor. Her mouth and nose covered, she walked toward it. Around the hole in the floor she saw the idols, standing guard the place of sacrifice. And inside...

She choked back a cry at the sight of the charred corpse of her baby, her unborn child, impaled on a spike and sitting atop the pyre. She screamed, and this time the sound came to her throat. The scream was the scream of all women from time immemorial, the scream of those who've had their young ripped from their bosom and even their wombs, those women who would never see the child grow to outlive them. And with that scream was put to rest the legacy of blood and anguish that had plagued that place, a centuries-old debt repaid.

She heard movement behind her and turned, and saw him creep up next to her her. The man with the melting face. And he was smiling.

THE WOMAN approached him where he sat under the black willow engaged at his task. It was dusk. Darkness had already come upon the swamp where they'd taken refuge.

—She has passed, the woman said.

His hand stilled, the knife resting on the raw antler in his palm. He nodded. She looked at him for some moments. When he did not speak, she turned and walked away.

The fire in the clearing behind him cast a light across one side of him, his shoulder and his cheek a fiery red, the color of dusk and the color of dawn. He looked at the small carving in his hand but gave no mind to the finishing of it, for the sculpture was already contained in the material and would reveal itself in due course. He thought of the woman and what she'd said to him only an hour before, knowing she was about to pass. And then, putting it from his thoughts, he scraped the knife over the antler in his hand, the shape of it coming to life: the claws and the beak, the eyes that saw all, the wings that soared high above the earth. Without haste and without effort, he released the bird from the bone, and when it was fully formed, he rubbed it down with pumice and oiled it and polished it, and when it was done he held it tightly in his hand.

When the women behind him had begun to mourn, he stood up and turned to the tent. He crossed the soft earth, and for the first time did not feel it speak to him, did not hear its whisper. The earth no longer communed with him. And it frightened him more than the fire and the sword.

He passed the women gathered around the fire and went into the tent. On the skin rug on the ground she lay, her eyes closed, and he saw with her passing that Kiehtan had departed and that the earth was now devoid of the great spirit and his power had left with him. He kneeled by the woman in final repose, put his hand on her breast and whispered: —*Matta neen wonckanet namen*. And he opened her hand and placed the idol into her hand and closed it. Perhaps it would carry her over.

When he'd wished her safe passage he went outside and kneeled by the fire and gazed into it, and with great grief in his heart, a heart that for the first time was parted from its maker and would never again be joined with it, said,

—I am Passaconaway. And I am the last.

END

Little Swine

A small basement cell. A dirty bed. A chair.

These are the confines of Little Swine's world. Prisoner of Momma and subject to the tortures of Boy, her life is a living hell.

Momma has a plan. Momma wants a baby that she may redeem the sins of her past. This is Little Swine's purpose. And when Momma has what she wants, Little Swine will be discarded.

But violence begets violence and blood begets blood, and many will die before the devil has his quota. One can never underestimate the power of retribution.

The Sistema Series

There is a company that provides a deeply sinister service for shady clients: subconscious torture for political or corporate manipulation. Vangelis Zervas is an agent of Vathos and does his job with zero qualms. But when a young boy is killed over a highly coveted piece of software that may have been produced by the company, the boy's mother goes in search of her son's killers. Meeting a group of disparate rebels with their own hostility toward Vathos, they join forces to bring down the company. Vangelis Zervas is on their radar, but will he see his way to help them and go rogue, or stay true to the devil inside? Sistema is a dystopian/cyberpunk horror that journeys into hell itself in

exploration of man's search for power and control.

MEAT

In the murky wake of the financial crisis a string of establishments pop up across Europe catering to a hedonistic underground, its clientele beholden to a strange, hallucinatory meat. Stoked by the fleshy and charismatic Hugo and fuelled by voracious consumption of ecstasy, the craze spreads from the heart of Europe all the way to the Mediterranean, where in Athens the financial elite begin to turn on each other. Murder, barbecue and apocalyptic raving ensues, culminating in the most savage party Mykonos has ever seen. Follow the story to its destructive end, where consumption eats itself alive.

NOTES FROM A CANNIBALIST

1847. Assuming the identity of a dead Jesuit priest, a survivor of the famine in Ireland travels to South America where he is tasked with rebuilding the missions among the natives. Inducted into local life, Father James Carmichael finds love with a native woman and becomes acquainted with the ways of the Guaraní, discovering ayahuasca and ritualism. In a battle with his own gods and demons, the priest fights for the life he envisions, his own self the ultimate stake of the struggle. Worlds are shattered, realities crumbled, lives destroyed. His soul victim to the crucible of the New World, what is tempered in the chaos will be outside his control.

A WHORE'S SONG

Hidden away in the backstreets of Amsterdam is a secretive whorehouse, open only to those in the know, where torture, pain and extreme sexual sport are the vehicle to understanding and self-knowledge. Run by the obscure Madame Zhu, the establishment is a magnet to the city's elite and mad soul-seekers alike. Two lives collide in a chaotic downward spiral brought about by psychoactives and sexual torture when, over the course of a day, a whore recounts her life as a destroyer of egos and one man is forced to face his deepest demons. Cast out into the far reaches of his mind, will he make it back from the other side?

In a world where the weak become prey and strength means brutality, living may come at the cost of dying first.

The Book of God

God has lost the plot. He spends his days in the trees killing birds, or crawling through the bushes to watch humans at their rut. His only companion and sole remaining attendant, a withered and tortured scribe, chronicles the Lord's descent into madness as he struggles to bring order to *The Book of Souls*, a record of every being that has ever passed and the reason for the Lord's suffering. But when the Scribe is forced to hire a maid to aid in the care of the Almighty, the introduction of a buxom woman into God's life brings chaos in its wake. Suffering rejection, humiliation and loathing of humankind, God seeks a way to bring back Christ and trigger the Apocalypse.

The Book of God is a work of prose, poetry and black humour that casts an irreverent eye on the holy trinity of sex, death and madness.

The Jaguar

1849. Salome Azul, daughter of a powerful politician, flees Buenos Aires at the height of the Argentinian civil war. In London she enlists the help of Irishman Sean Ryan to open The Nightingale, a high-class brothel and opium den that will be used to entrap and blackmail London's political elite.

In doing so she will make enemies. What's more, Ms. Azul has carried her own demons from Argentina, and it is these that will prove her most relentless foe. In order to survive, she must eliminate all weakness from her character. Doing so may mean cutting away all she cherishes most.

In the pursuit of power, unrelenting sacrifice is what decides who lives and dies.

WORKS OF TRANSLATION BY ULTAN BANAN

Pietro Aretino's Dialogues

Nanna has been a nun. She's been a wife. She has also been a courtesan. And now, as her daughter turns sixteen, she must decide how to advise on her path in life. On what route should she send young Pippa?

Bawdy, filthy, hilarious and uproarious, listen to Nanna regale her friend Antonia with scandalous tales—tales of seduction, blasphemy, lies, dishonesty, thievery, nastiness, cruelty and treachery—in an attempt to decide on what course to set her daughter: should she be a nun, a wife or a courtesan?

Ultan Banan started writing as a way of getting his head straight, discovering in the process that staying busy is the only way to stop oneself going insane. He devotes what time he can to writing, doing his best to avoid gainful employment by increasingly creative means. He lives on the move but dreams of a small cottage on a foul and inhospitable coast somewhere. Currently in Scotland.

Latest news at
ultanbanan.com

Substack:
ultanbanan.substack.com

Twitter:
twitter.com/ultanbanan